W9-CAP-619

THE BOY, THE BAKER,
THE MILLER and MORE

Also by Harold Berson

Henry Possum
Balarin's Goat
How the Devil Gets His Due

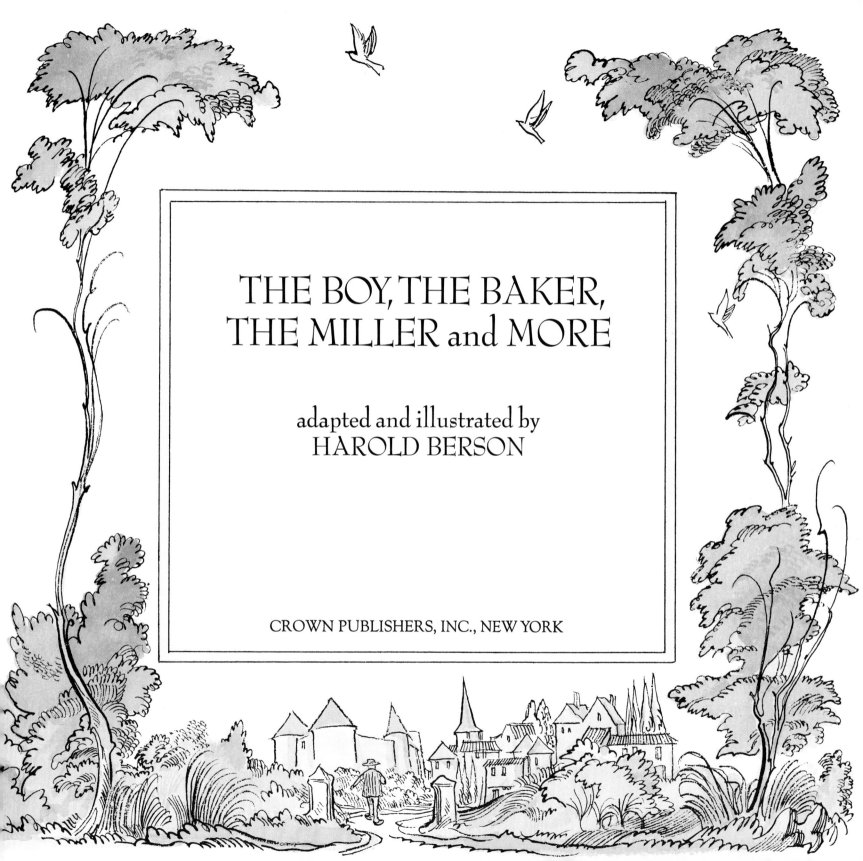

THE BOY, THE BAKER, THE MILLER and MORE

adapted and illustrated by
HAROLD BERSON

CROWN PUBLISHERS, INC., NEW YORK

Manufactured in the United States of America
Library of Congress Catalog Card Number: 72-96413
Published simultaneously in Canada by General Publishing
Company Limited
First Edition
The story is based on a French folk tale called Un Morceau de Pain.

The text of this book is set in 16 pt. Goudy Old Style.
The illustrations are 4/color pre-separated ink and wash drawings
with wash overlays, reproduced in halftone.

ONE MORNING a young boy walked into a bakery.
"I'm hungry," he said. "May I please have a piece of bread?"
"Of course," said the baker's wife, "but first you must get
the keys from the baker, for the bread is locked in the cupboard."

The little boy ran to the baker.

"Your wife will give me a piece of bread,"
he said, "if you will give me the keys
to the cupboard."
"Ah," said the baker, "I will give you

the keys if you will bring me a large ripe
apple, for I would like to make a tart."

The little boy went to find a gardener.
"May I have an apple from your tree?" he asked.
"I will give you an apple from my tree," he said,
"if you will bring me a cat to chase the mouse from my house.
He makes so much noise chasing about that I cannot sleep."

The little boy went to the fisherman who kept many cats.
"The gardener wants a cat," said the little boy. "May I have one of yours?"
"I will give you a cat," said the fisherman, "if you will bring him some milk to drink."

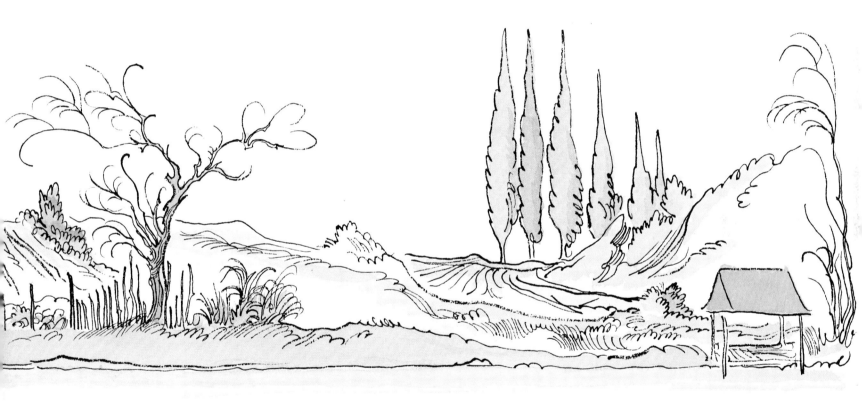

The little boy went to the barn and asked the milkmaid
for some milk. "I will gladly give you some milk," she said,
"if you will bring me some fresh sweet grass to feed my cow."

The little boy went to the village smith
and asked for a sickle to cut the grass
in the meadow.
"I will give you a sickle if you will
gather some wool from a sheep so that
I can line my coat for the winter."

The little boy went to the shepherd and asked him for wool from a sheep.

"I will give you wool if you will bring me a sack of grain to feed my sheep. The miller keeps it in his storehouse."

But the storehouse was locked.

The little boy looked around and saw the miller
sitting in front of his mill. "May I have a sack of
grain from your storehouse?" asked the little boy.
"The shepherd wants it for his sheep."
"If you can get it, you can have it," said the miller.
"I have lost the key and do not want to look for it right now."

The little boy went back to the storehouse and spied a ladder leading to an opened window.

He climbed up the ladder and through the window
and returned with a sack of grain.

He gave the grain to the shepherd. The shepherd gave the boy some wool from a sheep.

The boy gave the wool to the village smith.

The village smith gave the boy a sickle.

The boy cut fresh grass in the meadow.

He gave the
grass to the
milkmaid

who gave the
milk to the
little boy.

The little boy
gave the fisherman
some milk for
his cat.

The boy gave
the cat to the gardener

to chase the mouse
from his house.

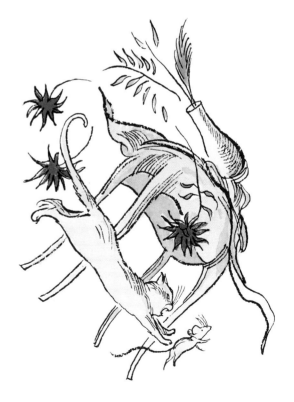

The gardener gave the
boy a large ripe apple
from his tree.

The boy gave the apple to the baker.

The baker gave him the key to the cupboard,

and the little boy gave the key to
the baker's wife. "What took you so
long to bring a mere key?" she asked.

"Well," said the little boy,

"to get the key
to the cupboard,

I needed an apple
from the gardener.

To get the apple
from the gardener,
I needed a cat.

To get a cat from the
fisherman, I needed
milk from a cow.

To get milk from a cow,
the milkmaid wanted
grass from the meadow.

To get grass from the
meadow, I needed a
sickle from the
village smith.

To get a sickle from
the village smith,
I needed wool from
a sheep.

To get wool from a
sheep, I needed grain
from the miller's
storehouse.

So…

I got the  from the miller's storehouse

and gave it to the shepherd. The shepherd gave me

the which I gave to the village smith and

he gave me the to cut the for the cow.

The milkmaid gave me some for the cat to chase

the from the gardener's house. The gardener gave

me an from his tree and I gave the to

the baker for his and then he gave me the .

That is why it took so long to get a mere key."

The baker's wife said nothing. She took the key and went to the cupboard.

As she was cutting
a thick slice of bread,

she saw that the boy had fallen asleep.
"Had I known I was sending you so far for so
little, I would have gotten the key myself."
And she went to the baker.

"Never should anyone have to work so hard for so little," she shouted.
"What are you talking about?" asked the baker.
And she told him.